The source of life is water
Without water we cannot live
Survive

As humans evolve
Expand
Move to different regions, we forget the importance of life
and water; the importance of keeping our waterways and
life clean.

This Earth is our source of life and we have to take care of
it. We have to maintain and sustain life for the better of
today and tomorrow.

MORGAN LYONS GILLFILLIAN

As I pay homage to my ancestry with the Morgan Lyons Gillfillian (Gilfillan) line of books, and although these books are fiction, from my mind; thought, I dedicate these books to truth, the truth of life, true living, our waterways, this earth, and the true love that I trust and doubt; Lovey.

There is no greater gift in life apart from truth and true love; water. Without truth you cannot live, and without truth you are nothing; you are a liar; thief; dead.

Further, as I think of Mother Earth and her beauty; all she has given me and humanity; I pay homage to her and all my true guides in the Spiritual Realm and physical realm. Without Earth and the Spiritual Realm, we cannot learn; nor can we survive. Both realms are within us, and both realms are a part of our life and life source; culture.

Earth maintains and sustains all life and for this, I have to thank Mother Earth as well as remember all the goodness she has and have given me and others.

Within this book there are no chapters, nor will there be in others. These books are a continuous flow of words; thoughts; my thoughts and words put in perspective for me and her; Earth, the Spiritual Realm and Higher.
Life is given and life is real.

We have to respect life; cherish life, and live. One cannot say, they have life and disrespect self and others; life on a whole.

Further, know that music is given in these books for you to comprehend and over stand my thoughts and me in some way. <u>***Each song given has and have a message, and it's up to you to overstand as well as comprehend the messages given.***</u> *Tomorrow does come, and it's up to you to live good and well today for you to enjoy tomorrow.*

As for me; I have to be proud of my heritage and who I am. I refuse to let anyone tell me to hate despite the words and undertone in these books, and the others I've written in the Michelle Jean line of books. I know who I am, and I am truly proud of me and the way God made me. So don't tell me to accept your heritage and call it mine.

Don't tell me to accept your god and gods and call it mine. I am truly not you, nor am I a part of your world and culture; false collection and false collective. Thus, keep your hate and pettiness; confused doctrine and doctrines.

These books are unconventional; nor do they comply with what you are used to. So keep an open mind, and enjoy me and my mind; the way I write at times.

MORGAN LYONS GILLFILLIAN

Contact info: morganlyonsgillfillian@gmail.com

"Quinten stop you are annoying me," getting upset at Quinten for distracting her from her studies; work. She needed to get her work done and with Quinten bugging her, she could not do what she needed to do; nor could she think properly.

"River, I need your help with this research."

"Quinten let Roxanne aide you. I have to study."

"River, you're the only one that can help me."

"Not right now," getting annoyed at Quinten. He was persistent; that annoying when he wanted to be.

"River come on," not giving up, he grabbed River's hand and pulled her with him. When he did that, River saw something; the past and she pulled away from him. "Please don't do that." She was scared and it showed in her face. What she saw was not pleasant.

"River are you alright?"

"I don't know," and she fainted. When she woke, she was laying in the Professor's office.

"What am I doing here?" Fully awake and noticing her surroundings.

"You fainted and Quinten brought you here."

"Why? I was perfectly fine in my dorm room."

"Were you?" The Professor asked doubtingly. He was concerned about the well being of River but helpless to help her when it came to her visions.

"Professor, I'm the one with the unexplained visions. Visions that are haunting me, visions I am seeing about the past. Visions that are deadly because I saw an entire civilization wiped out because of White People and their greed and lust for power, wealth, money, control, and domination." And, *AMBUSH IN THE NIGHT by Robert Nesta Marley aka Bob Marley* chimed in. There was so much darkness; death and she could not explain it. The blood, gore, starvation, pestilence, whoredom, confusion, hate and lies; deceit she could not tolerate or take anymore. So called civilization had gone too far with death and destruction; the annihilation of all, and with Quinten touching her; bringing her back to the past history of man was not what she wanted to see. His touch was her ambush because he took her back to a world she did not want to see or relive; a world of pain and horror; the truth of so called civilization.

"River, I know the White Race has and have not been kind to others, but we are not all bad; evil. Not all kill."

"From what I see Professor, I beg to differ. Your delusional history and lies speaks volumes for itself. Many people have and has died over the centuries because of the White Race and their lies. Many lost their homes and land because of White People. Many have died from their diseases; lust to steal what does not belong to them. Billions more will die because of the false doctrines they give and preach globally."

"River, I know what you see, but I am not like that," said the Professor and Quinten went to sit beside her. Holding her hand River once again saw the past of old. This time it was Whites slaughtering Whites; those of a different hue, and eye colour, and River quickly pulled her hand away from Quinten.

Getting up she almost fainted and the Professor rushed to her side. The brutality was too fierce for her. She had never seen so much evil from one race of people before, and her mind went into overload and overdrive. How could one race of people be so evil and without mercy for their own? How could humans slaughter each other like that River thought? Was life not of concern to them? Did they even know about true life? Everyone is given life and it's up to each individual to live accordingly. But for some, the select few, you could not live your way; you had to live their way, live by their laws, their restrictions; what they say; tell you.

"Quinten please don't touch me ever again." Pulling away from the Professor she left his office without saying another word. She could not see any more death because it was playing havoc on her health. It made her body weak; tired and drained.

"Professor what did I do?"

"You trigger something in her Quinten. She's seeing the past, the unpleasant and destructive path of the White Race."

"Professor, I want to shield her from all that pain. She cannot keep going back in the past Professor. I need her to see the future, the people we've become. We have hope and a future Professor, and I need her to see this and not see the negative side of our past. Yes we are brutal, but the future belongs to us. We are the chosen."

"But she's seeing the horrors of the past Quinten. Now tell me this; does the past not dictate the future to a certain extent? Can sin change for the better Quinten? Can a nation of murderers bring forth truth and goodness? How many more civilization must be wiped out; become extinct for us to realize war, hate, strife, killing, death is not the answer to life and our problems that we face? And if we were the chosen; why do we hate and kill; take life from life?"

"Professor you talk as if all in the White Race is evil."

"And what has the history of the White Race dictated over the different ages; lifetimes and centuries?"

"But you're White Professor."

"Am I truly White Quinten?"

"Professor stop speaking in riddles, your hue is White that makes you White."

"When have I based my life on the colour of my skin Quinten?"

"Never"

"Hence the difference between me and you." Quinten could not comprehend what the Professor was talking about when it came to hue; the colour of one's skin.

"But what about River Professor?"

"She is going back into the past Quinten. She will eventually find out the truth. You must tell her who she is and who you are to her."

"I can't Professor."

"Then lose her again. She trusted you then, let her trust you now."

"I have to protect her. I have to protect her from the past."

"Protecting her does not mean keeping secrets from her Quinten. She's an intricate part of our life; so tell her the truth."

"I can't Professor. I too have a job to do, and as much as I love River, I have to get her to see things my way," and

Quinten smiled. The Professor he could talk to and rely on. He was there for him through thick and thin as well as his voice of reasoning. Seeing the lightning from a distance the Professor knew what that meant.

"We have to get her to safety Quinten." Death loomed; walked. Now death was ready to take the flesh of humans on a massive scale.

"I know." Going after River Quinten caught up with her as soon as she was about to enter her dorm.

"Quinten go away."

"I can't River; it seems I trigger something in you."

"You do Quinten. I do not want to see any more pain and suffering; death."

"Then trust me."

"I cannot lead you there Quinten. I truly do not want to go back into the past. It's dangerous; you of all people know this. Therefore, the past must stay in the past."

"I know the past is dangerous, but think of the technology; think of the good we can do today with this technology."

"They died because of their technology; resources Quinten. Some had to flee earth leaving family members behind. They the ancients left so many resources on earth; now humans have destroyed it all. So no, I will not take you back into the past to further corrupt and pollute the future. What's done is done." River knew the technology of the ancients; the unlimited power they possessed to create a new, but she could not lead Quinten there. She could not let that power fall into the wrong hands.

"River, think of the possibilities. We can revitalize earth once again. We can give her new life; a new and better beginning. Shit with this new power we can create a new earth. Truly think River."

"We cannot change or alter the past Quinten. Humans are barbarians. They kill; take life from life Quinten."

"River, we don't have to change the past. We can take today; the here and now with us."

"We cannot change or undo what has been done Quinten. Humans need to pay the cost; penalty for their evil actions. I will not save humanity because humanity cannot change. They refuse to abide by the laws of life therefore; they are killing self and this planet."

"There's a safe haven River."

"Yes there is, but that safe haven is no more. The ancient ones made sure they destroyed that key before they left."

"That was selfish on their part."

"Are humans not selfish and wicked? Did humans think of their future and preserving their future? Do they not consume and kill? Do they not take without remorse? Are they not killing; destroying the home and planet they live in? Are they not eroding life daily?"

"Earth cannot die River."

"No it cannot. She will rebuild herself but it's going to take a while. Plus she cannot do it with humans killing her daily. She too have to think of herself and her life; what it takes to replenish and build her in a positive and true way. As Mother Earth, she can no longer cry for wicked and evil humans and what they do to her, self and others. She can no longer give the wicked and evil a home in her; nor can she continue to shield them from death. The wicked and evil respect her not, so they deplete her resources without thinking about the lasting effect and the damage they are doing to her. She knows that there isn't another planet like her that can house, sustain and maintain life; physical and spiritual life at the same time despite the lies the people that are in the space programs globally feed and tell society. *Earth was designed for a purpose thus; no one dies on earth; they die someplace else.*"

"Humans do not know these things River.

"No they do not."

"Then have mercy on her; Earth."

"The earth needs not my mercy Quinten. She will be fine. It's humans that need mercy now. Humans play God; want to be God but yet, cannot control self; the greed and evil that they live for. Many are not satisfied, so they manipulate and kill others then; call it survival."

"But yet you are amongst them."

"Not by choice Quinten and you know this."

"Then help me to save them."

"I cannot, because humans are barbaric; barbarians that cannot live in peace. The council have my report Quinten and I will not change it to please you or anyone."

"I am pleading for humanity River."

"Yes you are. But in pleading for humanity, who is pleading for earth and the waters of earth? In pleading for humanity, who will plead for you Quinten? Have humans not polluted everything? Have humans not caused trees, waterways, animals to become extinct? Now they are causing earth to die; to become extinct. Have humans not diminished her life and resources?"

"Yes but forgiveness."

"Has and have been written out of the Book of Life for those who are wicked and evil. Evil cannot be forgiven for the sins they do continually Quinten and you know this.

Just as humans have a right to live; so does life. Life has a right to live, but not in evil and sufferation; the dominion and domination inflicted on them by others. No one can live if they are given death Quinten, thus; life, the life in, and the life of life must reject death. Truth is life and lies are death."

"Yes life is worth it and life is the key, but I will not allow you to cause billions to die River."

"I did not cause this Quinten. Humans caused it upon self. Humans took away from their life thus humans are the ones to blame. Humans were given messengers; true messengers but they rejected them. Were humans not told to reject the evil systems of death in Babylon System by Robert Nesta Marley aka Bob Marley? Did he Bob Marley not tell them; all he had was redemption songs in Redemption Song? Music was his tool and truth that he was given to teach humanity by. Did humans listen? When Marcus Mosiah Garvey was sent to liberate them from the blindness of mental and physical slavery, did they listen? **Was he not set up by others and his own?** *You plead for humanity but yet, forget that Death had time to take people. You forget that those who had not life, knew they were going to die at the hands of death did deceive many; made the many their sacrifice unto death in hopes that they would gain life and favour from death. But with all; none can gain favour and life from death. Hence the people in this world are confused, delusional, liars, thieves, murderers and so much more. You've forgotten that humans say they want saving and when saviours; messengers are sent to them, they*

reject these messengers for death. **So, humans cannot be loyal to life, they can only be loyal to death because death is their beginning and end."**

"River, humans need you to survive."

"Yes, but the survival of humans is truly not my concern, nor is the survival of humans up to me. Humans had a choice and they did choose. I will not stop their choice. I will not undo the choice and choices they've made for self, each other and their family including friends and foes."

"What if they changed?"

"Humans cannot change Quinten. Humans' desire, lust, kill, control, steal, dominate, lie, die. The life humans live is due to choice. Their choice and the choice of their ancestors. Therefore, some live by false traditions and lies; false traditions and lies that they hand down to their children from generation unto generation to further take future generations from life. These traditions and lies, I cannot go against because they are choices made as well as handed down from family member to family member and yes others."

"With all that said River, let me prove you wrong. I will show you that humans can change."

"I cannot go against life and time Quinten. I cannot extend the time of humans. Humans were given time to change, but they went against time. They did nothing to preserve their future for self and future generations; including preserving this earth for self and future generations."

"You can extend the time of humans River. Give me one day."

"I'm sorry I cannot. ***Humans already had a day, and they did not use this day wisely.*** " She was about to close the door on Quinten when he pushed his way in.

"Please go Quinten."

"I cannot River."

"I know the past, present, and future Quinten. I know of my trust when it comes to you but I cannot trust you anymore. You speak of saving a species that are murderous. Tell me. What have you learned over the years and centuries when it comes to humans? You saw the brutality of men. You saw children die senselessly, you saw children being raped and robbed of their dignity. You saw the nudity, the nakedness of many, the whoredom of males and females, but yet you plea for a race that have no dignity or mercy when it comes to life and the life of others."

"I know what you are saying River, but I've learnt that humans are misguided and confused. They do not know the truth, nor do they have proper direction."

"And with all that they know and do; have they truly sought the truth? Have they sought proper direction?"

"No, and that's because they don't know where to look."

"Do they not have a heart?"

"Yes"

"So how could they not know where to look?"

"They did not have the right teachers."

"Were you not here with them?"

"Yes"

"Could you not have taught them?"

"Yes"

"So why didn't you?' And she turned from him. Receiving the lightning bolt and water droplet, she turned to Quinten and said; 'this is the life of humanity."

"It's faded; dim." Surprised that the lives of humans had faded so much over the years and centuries.

"Yes"

"Please save them."

"I cannot," and she closed her hand and eyes and Quinten rushed to hug her. Opening her eyes she fell to the ground.

"I cannot let you take the lives of billions. They deserve to live." He wasn't ready to give up hope on humanity. To Quinten, humans could change; do better. But in all that Quinten did and thought; he did not see that he was deceiving himself.

Humans had time but none amended their past; sought to pay off the debts and sins of their ancestors; debts that are handed down from generation unto generation. Debts that are still on record until this day. Therefore, the sins of the fathers and mothers fall on their children and future generations; thus generational sins pass on through the blood and bloodline of humans.

Quinten did not realize that all unpaid debts are files that are still on record; still unpaid; owing. Humans did change over the centuries not for the better but for the worse. Now look at the world and what humans have and has become. Humans did become devils; the ones to go down to death and die. They were the ones to destroy it all; so they keep fighting; kill to preserve death and not life; their own life and living. Now all hope had faded for them. They could not dance anymore, could not vibe; truly love. They walked in sin; basked in the delicacies of sin thus; that one drop of hope was taken from the many. *One Drop Robert Nesta Marley aka Bob Marley.*

Waking up, River found herself in a padded room. Quinten had stopped her. He was going to change time no matter the cost and consequence to him and humans. In all he did, he was going to save humanity; extend the time of humans so that they can save themselves. But in all Quinten thought, he failed to realize that life cannot stay with death. Life can no longer live amongst the death of life. Life had to be taken from the living, breathing and walking dead.

Knowing something was wrong, the Professor rushed to the aide of River but he was too late. Quinten had her contained in one of the labs. She could not escape if she tried.

"Quinten you cannot do this," the Professor said. He was concerned for the safety and well being of River.

"Professor I have to. I love her, but I cannot let her take the lives of billions. Humans deserve to live. They have a right to life. River can save humanity but won't. So since she refuses to save humanity; then I will. Despite the flaws of them; humans, they can change."

"You cannot go against the will of humans Quinten."

"I am not Professor. I am saving them. I am giving them life; a fighting chance."

"How? By you keeping River in that cell, she will die."

"So be it. Humans can change. I rather her die than humanity; humans."

"Quinten, humans made a choice. River is not the one to kill humanity, humans did that by themselves. They went against the laws of life. They sinned. They destroyed the home that was given to them thus severing their lifeline with life; God."

"Humans don't know this Professor. We do, but they don't. River can change the laws of life. She is River; the source of all life. She brings forth life. She's a part of the foundation of life because she's Black."

"She's not the source of all life Quinten because not everyone hath life. And despite her being Black and from the foundation of life, she cannot go against life."

"She is the source of life, she can change things. I am going back. I will change it all you'll see," defiant to the end.

"You cannot change history Quinten."

"I can Professor. You've been around me for centuries. I gave humanity a chance."

"They did not accept that chance Quinten."

"They will now knowing that they are going to die."

"Quinten, how many have come before you imploring humanity; humans to change their dirty and unclean ways, and they did not listen? The wages of sin is death. They know this but yet, choose to die due to their sins."

"Professor I have faith in them."

"How can you when they have no faith in themselves. They live to die instead of living to live. Quinten think. Are you willing to die for them?"

"No Professor, but if I can give them the time they need; that time extension, then I will with or without the permission of the council."

"Quinten, the ancients will not allow you to change time nor alter the course of history for people who care not for their own lives; safety."

"They will have no other choice. I have one of their own. They will have to listen to me."

"Quinten what's gotten into you? You know the rules."

"Rules are meant to be broken Professor."

"Quinten"

"Professor nothing you say will change my mind. I love them too much to see them die."

"Do not open that portal Quinten."

"I have to Professor." Opening the Portal of Time Quinten stepped inside. He needed to save humanity. He needed them for him and his plans. Seeing the dismay on the Professor's face Quinten said; 'Professor come with me."

"I cannot Quinten. I cannot go against life. I cannot go against River."

"Professor you can't protect her anymore. It's over. She's going to die."

"Then let me die alongside her."

"As you wish," and Quinten was gone closing the portal to their time and defying life.

Quinten did all for humanity but humanity did nothing for him. He could not see that humanity was beyond saving. Humanity had no respect for life, so life could not respect them. Life had to leave humanity to their own choosing; downfall. It was beyond River how people say they wanted and needed saving but did nothing to save themselves. It was beyond reasoning how death became a norm in the lives of humans. Love to them meant; hate, hurt and pain; lies. So how can lives be saved, if humans had no self worth and value; self respect?

How can humans be saved if death is a part of their lives and DNA?

Should one not break away from sin and death, and do all that is good and true for self and others?

"I made sure she cannot escape Professor." The Professor heard as the portal closed.

"River," rushing to her containment unit.

"River speak to me."

"I can't because I've failed."

"He had to do what he had to do River."

"Then get me out." And at that moment the Professor let water into her containment unit and River was free.

"He opened a portal to time."

"Then let him be."

"River"

"I will not stop him Professor; I have to let him be. He made his choice to die alongside them; humans."

"He's going to change the future, the present and the past."

"No one can change the present or the past Professor. Humans determine their own path and pathway; future, not him, not me, not you and definitely not the ancients or the council of life."

"I don't understand."

"The DNA of man cannot be changed in the physical realm Professor you know this."

"Yes I do."

"So then let's leave it at that. The choice of man; humans is the choice of man; humans."

"He loved you you know."

"He loved himself Professor. The strength and power I have is his desire. The strength and power you have is his desire. He wants to rule humans **but not even humans can rule themselves.** The greed and lies of the many will always take precedence over the lives of the chosen few."

"Man cannot see beyond the greed of self; thus the dead in life cannot have life nor enter into our realm."

"Yes. So, shall we go home?"

"Not yet."

"Professor"

"River"

"Mammi awaits us my darling so let's go home."

"He was my friend River."

"Professor, he was never your *true friend*. You taught him many things but you cannot give the dead life, nor can you bring the dead back to life."

"He opened the portal River."

"Yes, but to where?"

"River he was supposed to protect you."

"But over time greed consumed him. The technology of the past ancients he wanted; need to have control."

"I wanted the same thing too River, but the suffering, hurt, and pain that I saw, I did not want. I do not want to control or dominate River. I need to be free. I need people, our children and their off springs to be free. We both know hell. You are not in hell thus life and death is separated. Those that go down to hell must burn and cannot quench their thirst until their time is served; they fade away and become indefinitely extinct. River I need you and when you are gone we are left for dead; we die."

"Because of life our children and their offspring's cannot and will not die, hence the different life we bring forth; give birth to through Mother Earth. Life cannot die Professor because death is not in our genes; DNA hence we have no hue in our purest of form."

"True"

"Professor"

"Shh because I am glad you are my wife."

"But he loved me."

"He cannot have what I have. You are my Black Goddess with the coolest and most beautiful brown skin. You are also the giver of life and the bearer of life."

"Professor"

"You are truth River."

"Thank you," hugging her husband.

"Enough with the formalities; let's go you two," they heard Mammi say.

"Mammi"

"Now," and the two held hands and they were gone.

"Mammi"

"You are both safe."

"Thank you."

"You're both decontaminated hence the hue is gone. You are pure."

"But Quinten?"

"Is safe in his world. The world of his choice; disobedience and despair; death."

"Can we help him?"

"There is a great divide my child. We cannot enter into his realm nor can they come to ours. Good and Evil are separated you know this."

Is there a key to unlock his realm and let them come into ours Mammi?" River asked.

"That key is life child. If you have not life, you cannot enter into our realm; kingdom."

"Mammi, why do certain people live to control and dominate? Why is greed all that some see?"

"Child, I cannot tell you because I am not them. I've never lived an unclean life."

"But why do we have to go amongst them?"

"Because of Earth. She too needs to be saved and whether you like it or not, we are a part of her."

"But she says nothing Mama. She's hurting but humans cannot see this. They can't see the value and beauty of her; so they do all to destroy her little by little day by day."

"I know my child but you my child is gone from humanity; the wicked and evil of earth and the spiritual realm; including gone from their land and lands. The waters of Earth will no longer maintain and sustain them; the wicked and evil. Earth's waters must turn against humanity due to sins; the sins of humans. And as time moves on; tell, the waters of Earth must be like Bitter Gaul unto humans; the wicked and evil of the lands. *(Time Will Tell Robert Nesta Marley aka Bob Marley.)* As the wicked and evil has and have destroyed the waterways of life, the waterways of life, the trees of life, the breath of life, the sand and seas; ground must become like them; lifeless; void of all things good and pure. *You cannot say you want life and do all to hurt and destroy life.* We have life; hence we are the waters of life. They (humans) have death because death was their choice. You took the waters of life from them. Now all must be a part of the fires of death; hell."

"But the wars throughout the different centuries Mammi; the slavery, the hurt and pain. Women did become whores and prostitutes to men. Men did put themselves as the head of the household; men did abuse women and children. Men caused humanity to bow down to death, and look at the chaos that ensued. Innocent people died. Innocent people are still dying and suffering at the hands of the wicked and evil."

"Ah my child, you see and know differently. Not all that dies is innocent. Many are evil. Good cannot die and you know this."

"But the wars and loss Mammi."

"Did not have to be child. If humans had wanted life they would have accepted life, but they didn't. They chose death, so death takes them; take many of them to their world to die. We cannot interfere. They are cut off from us due to choice. Know that, you did not kill them; they killed self. Good can no longer maintain and sustain the wicked and evil. The council has spoken. Not one of us can go against the will of man; humans no matter how painful it is for us."

"But can we stop it Mammi?"

"We cannot. Once the choice of a human has been made, it's recorded and they; that person must live with the choice they have made. Listen child, evil cannot be good no matter how good they say they are. Once evil is engrained in your physical and spiritual DNA, you cannot change it. Therefore, neither good nor evil can live in peace and true peace with each other."

"Papa, the Professor heard his daughter say as he stood listening to mother and daughter talk."

"Hey my daughter," hugging his little droplet. She was as beautiful and clear as him. Crisp and cool.

"Daddy, I can bring forth droplets now."

"You have to show me."

"Come," and his daughter led him away from Mammi and River.

"Be happy."

"I am Mammi."

"Know that you didn't fail Quinten, Quinten, failed Quinten."

"I was not sent to save him."

"Nor were you sent to save the world. *The waters of earth must change; recede child. You did your job, you took you from humans.*"

"I know but you can't help rooting for them in hopes that they would change."

"But if people are happy the way they are, why want to change them?"

"But not all are happy Mammi."

No, hence no one look at the choices they make in life. Every negative choice you make affects you, others, and this earth because Earth is a part of life."

"They are distracted Mammi."

"Distraction is not an excuse child. We've all had to make choices in our lives. Did you not make your choice to stay true to life? Did Quinten not give you a choice and you stayed true? Did your husband not stay true to you?"

"Yes, but for some it's hard because we are not there for them. We leave them to suffer. How many are trying to find their way and are left by the wayside to die; feel pain and sorrow?"

"True, but have you looked at their ancestral history; the sins of their forefathers and mothers."

"But not all, nor should any be judged based on their ancestral history Mammi."

"Not all is, hence some are with us. They stayed true to life no matter the persecution and pain. Life cannot deny life child you know this."

"I do, but it hurts."

"My child, come into my arms,' and she did. 'Truth cannot lie. His love was not true. Clean cannot live for the unclean, nor can truth deceive. Quinten was never true. He wants power and control. Wanted to rule humans. Life, life cannot rule anyone my child. Life can only grow good, true and free; hence life goes up not down."

"I know these things Mammi."

"Then know that there are no rulers in life. This humans' have not figured out for self. Control leads to hate and deceit."

"I know this Mammi."

"Then do not feel sorry for Quinten or humans. Earth will rise again. She will be free from the evils of men; humans. She's ready and time is with her, " Mammi smiled and chimed in **Rise Again by Mr. Vegas** to help her heal her hurt and pain. Earth too needed healing from the pain and sufferings humans inflict on her daily. She needed true rest, comfort, from her hurt and pain.

"I can't help it. Despite his warped thinking Mammi, I can't help thinking about him and what he wanted to do in regards to saving humans, and extending their time on earth."

"And what good would he have done to extend the time of humans? Baby girl, it's not all about humans, we have to think about the life; earthly life and spiritual life. Evil cannot continue on its path and journey of destruction. Evil must be stop. So once again, what good would Quinten have done to extend the time of humans?"

"I don't know."

"Child, extending the time of humans will only make them suffer even more."

"But are they not going to suffer in hell?"

"Baby girl, those that want and need saving will be saved due to them changing their dirty ways and finding the truth. And this is if evil is not engrained in their physical and spiritual DNA. Know that true life has nothing to worry about because they are already saved. My child', smiling beautifully at River Mammi was proud of her daughter and how obedient she was to life. 'Know that life has nothing to do with death. From you accept death as your lord and saviour, your God, your commission, your sacrifice; you cannot be saved, you are going to die."

"Mammi I can't help the way I feel, you want better for them you know, and River held back her tears."

"I know, but right now, humans can change the course of their fate. Our time is not the same as human time, so humans still have a chance. You taking yourself away from them now can change. Life is dependent on life child not death. Life cannot kill or destroy, nor can life take life from life."

"But yet I still feel for them; those that are not saved."

"Tell me something, do you love your husband?"

"No, I do not love him. We are true; hence my truth is true love and I truly love him. We are devoted to each other despite the past, and all that humans have put us through."

"Then live my child. *Never want dirty or feel sorry for dirty.* Your heart is pure, let it stay pure."

"Wow," feeling the water droplet.

"She's come a long way,' seeing father and daughter walking back to them. 'Baby we are alive truly live."

"Yes Mam."

"Good girl."

"No, this can't be happening. I came back in time to change time." Quinten was confused. He had set the time line and he was nowhere near the time zone he'd set. He was in a different place speaking to someone he knew all too well.

"No one can change time Quinten, you should know that."

"River made time stand still."

"River did not make time stand still. Time is time and there are different times and time zones."

"Time stood still. I saw River change time. Time was going fast as if out of breath, and she stopped time." Getting annoyed at the person he was talking to.

"Which time Quinten?"

"What?" Confused. And Death put his hand around Quinten and said "welcome home brother."

"Why has my hue changed, and why am I white; their colour?

"You were always their colour. You just didn't notice it; could not see the man in you."

"But I have life."

"If you had life you would not be here, you would be there with River and her family."

"But I came back in time. I have the key to time."

"You could not have had the key to time Quinten because I was with you everywhere you went. Hence you are here with me due to choice."

"How?' Confused. 'I cannot be here, something is wrong. This is not my time and place. I should not be here," getting upset and paranoid. He was not supposed to be in hell but there he was, in hell and looking paranoid and confused; disillusioned.

"But you are here. Your actions led you here. You made the choice to go against life, hence all who disobeys life ends up here."

"But there's so many people."

"Yes"

"They are in misery. Where is River; the rivers of water?

"There is none here. The Rivers of Water cannot abide here because this is not their realm. This is my realm; the realm of fire; death."

Looking around dazed and confused Quinten could not believe there was no water where he was. The place was barren; like the desert; without growth; just dry. "There has to water here. I locked River away for safe keeping. I need to get out of here. I have to go back in time. I have to bring her here because no one can survive without water; the waters of life."

"You cannot go back in time Quinten. You are where you are supposed to be. No one leaves here when they come here. This is my realm; the realm of death and darkness, pain and suffering."

"Impossible, this isn't hell, the hell I know."

"No, this is the true hell; the hell that was kept from humans; all of humanity. Here is where your spirit comes to die for different lifetimes. Hence water is taken from the spirit and fire is given."

"What!" Shocked at what Death said.

"Depending on your sin many will burn for trillions of years. See,' holding Quinten closer to him. *'Each sin has a price associated to it.* Hence the time of man is not the time of God and Death. I rule here, and I need to be entertained." Smiling as he talked to Quinten. For Death, Quinten was right where he need and wanted him to be, because he now had another lost soul in his midst. Another lost soul that is going to keep him alive a little bit longer.

"Hearing the wails and cries of the spirit of humans entertain (s) you?" Quinten asked in disbelief.
Laughing Death said, "no, the wails, cries, pain and suffering entertain my demons. They live and breathe pain, hence they were bred for torment, tormenting the soul and spirit of the wicked and evil. See Quinten, demons cannot torment the soul and spirit of the good and true. Those people are not my people, nor can I torment them. But, the wicked and evil; all who do evil, is mine to do what I want and please when they get here."

"But there are so many people here."

"And billions more will join you shortly because billions made the choice to die. They chose lies over Good, hence their false beliefs and beliefs, false hope, false prophets, false beginnings, false history, the false life they live; thus their false ending that leads them here."

"I failed," in disbelief.

"Yes you did, because you cannot change the course of history; humans. Humans decide for self, not the other way around. Thus the difference between life and death."

"I am not dead. I have life. I was amongst life and I saw what life can do. I saw life bring forth life."

"Yes you did, but could you give life? Could you bring forth life like River and the Professor; her husband?" Death asked Quinten because in everything Quinten thought he knew, he knew nothing; nor did he learn anything about goodness and truth; good value, self worth and self respect of self and others from being around River and the Professor. In all Quinten did; greed, power, and control blinded him and took him further away from life.

"The Professor is not her husband. And yes, I could bring forth life. It was only a matter of time," Quinten said and Death laughed at him.

Suddenly Death stopped laughing and asked; "can the dead bring forth life Quinten?"

"Anyone can bring forth life."

"The dead cannot bring forth life Quinten. The dead need life to give them life and bring forth life. The dead need the soul and body of the good and true. Once good bonds with evil through sexual intercourse, and a child is conceived then evil is born; given life on earth."

"That's impossible, I have life. I am of life."

"But you are dead. You are in the valley of the dead; Hell," and Quinten screamed, "NO." He could not believe he was deceiving himself all along. He watched River and the Professor.

He learned so much from them but in the end, he was the deceived; the one that was not true.

THE END

FOOTNOTE

The word Mammi is a Swedish dessert but that is not why I used the name Mammi in this book. I used Mammi because Maami is a Jamaican word for Mother.

Know that the name Mammi is taken from root word Mami Wata, the African Goddess or God of water.

As we know, water is the source of all life whether physical or spiritual. This is why it's important to keep our waterways clean and pure. Without water or Wata we would not exist. So let's cherish our Wata; Mothers of the Earth including self.

Further, as dependents on the different eco systems of life; we need water to sustain and maintain us, and if we lose Wata or our waterways, we will be doomed; perish. Respect is due therefore, I pay homage to Mammi; the Waters of Life in this way; through words. Thus know that the beginning of life is not flesh but water, and the true gift of life is not money but water. When you pray and ask God to bless you, he blesses you with water. Therefore, God's blessing and greatest gift apart from truth is abundant on earth through the form of water, Earth's greatest and most pure and natural resource. So know the importance and significance of water in both realms.

MLG

YOSEF AND ANGELIQUE

In you I will trust
Abide
Help

I will be there for you
Be true
Committed
Free

As we share our life together
I will keep my pledge to you

I will honour you,
I will stay true, and if I lose my way; I will find myself back to you.

mlg

Finding the right balance in life is truly not easy especially when it comes to love and true love; affairs of the heart. There is no balance in love but then again, true love is rare thus many live for love and not truth; true love.

For Angelique, Yosef was different. He truly loved her and she him but when tragedy struck, Angelique opted to walk. She did not stay; could not handle the pressure. Talking was not an option, so she ran like the wind without looking back. Yosef was her boss but not even his love for her could save them.

It had been years since she left and now she was back working for him.

Getting away for two weeks Angelique was having fun with Brent. She did not love him, they were just sex; casual sex with no strings attached.

Brent was good looking and charming but that was it; nothing else for Angelique. Intellectually, he was not on Angelique's level. He could not comprehend what she did and Angelique did not want him to either. She wasn't into him that way.

Lying on her stomach in bed Brent sat beside her and rubbed her naked back. He had enjoyed the love they shared and wanted more. Of all the women he had been with, Angelique was the only one that could satisfy him sexually. He had a big appetite for her and she fulfilled it in ways he didn't think possible.

I want more of you you know."

"I know," she said smiling and not looking at him. She was still on her stomach relishing in the thought of their sexual escapade. She had also been avoiding her phone for the past day and a half. Now the urgent call came and she had to pick up. She knew who it was and the reason for the call but she wanted to be reckless a little bit longer in her sexual exploits with Brent. He was that greedy for sex with her, and she was up for the challenge especially seeing him try so hard to make her cum with him.

Taking a deep breath she said; "Brent hold that thought." Answering her cell phone she heard, "don't let me come and get you," barked the angry Yosef.

"Yosef, I am on leave," she calmly said. As of late he was short tempered and angry. But can you blame him seeing the woman that captured his heart in every which way savouring the juices of another man. Oh how he yearned and craved Angelique but another claimed her; was enjoying the warmth of her.

"Your leave is over. I will be at the airport in less than an hour, so I suggest you be there when I get there."

"Listen"

"No, you listen. Now Angelique," Yosef barked louder and hung up the phone on her. Rolling on her back she did not have a pleased look on her face and Brent knew she had to go.

"Have to go?"

"Yes"

"That serious that you can't postpone?"

"That serious that I can't postpone," smiling at him and he lowered his head and kissed her. Stopping him before things could escalate she got out of bed.

"I have to go." Getting a quick shower Angelique dressed in jeans and t-shirt, got her small bag and purse and was out the door with Brent. There sex-capade had come to an end at the behest of her irate boss.

"Call me when you have time."

"I will and, if you don't hear from me; know it's something truly serious and I can't get away."

"In that case I will call; text if I can't get you."

"You do that," hugging Brent she saw Yosef in the distance. "I have to go," and she was gone like a school girl on punishment.

When she approached Yosef she said; "couldn't this have waited Yosef?" And he uttered not a word. His silent treatment was his way of saying I am going to chew you out when we are alone. He was that angry and she knew it.

She knew his talk, his feel; his world. It was different, and she was the only one he let in on that scale. He trusted and relied on her that much but with her being with Brent, changed him for the worst Angelique thought. She knew he did not like her seeing Brent but he said nothing to her. It was her life and she was living it. Just the silent treatment of Yosef alone made her miss Brent. All they did was have sex and she liked the sex he gave. His shortness of time was what she needed for now. He did his best to make sure you cum with him, but Angelique was different. No matter how hard he tried, no matter how many times they had sex for the day, he could not get her to cum with him. She tired him out, and for the week she was with him, he was tired. Although she cooked and cleaned he was tired. He was the type of person that did his best to please you, but that heightened sexual explosion Angelique needed, he did not have. Finding the right spot within her he could not do; find and, faking orgasms Angelique was not into. She rather liked the way Brent tried to make her cum, but could not no matter how hard he tried.

Going home Brent's apartment felt empty. His frig was full, apartment spotless, clothes neatly put away, even his bills was up to date. There was no slouching with Angelique apart from sexually. She made him slouch sexually; did not pressure him when he could not go or give her the more she needed.

She was perfect, but he did not fit into her world. She was technical and hands on, and to her knowledge base, she did not bring him into her world. He did not understand her, nor could he figure out her world; so she made him feel as comfortable as possible. She did not speak of her world to him because it was like comparing apples to oranges, and explaining why oranges have rind in its skin and apples did not. Both fruits work in the same way, but are totally different in other ways. *(Health benefits)*

Although her world was different from Brent's she knew his world but stayed away from it. He had his own company, but she did not pry. Their relationship was not that way. Their relationship was sex and only sex. Sex he Brent was up for and got.

Feeling uncomfortable and in need of a change of clothing Angelique got up. Her attire was not befitting for her surroundings but then, she was not expecting Yosef to come get her. She was on a sexual getaway and sex she got when she wanted and how she wanted it, no matter the brief intervals of Brent.

Making her way to the bedroom Yosef followed her, grabbed her and pushed her into the door. Lifting her up she could see the anger, hurt and pain in his eyes, and she calmly said; "put me down Yosef."

"Why?" He barked.

"This is my personal life Yosef and not yours, so I suggest you put me down," and he did. Yanking every piece of clothing off her body Angelique stood naked before him. Getting her attire Yosef laid her clothes on the bed. Angelique was still in awe as to what Yosef did. He had never been physical with her in that way before. But then again, she was seeing someone; someone he did not like nor did he think was the right one for her educationally, sexually, physically or emotionally.

Still speechless, at the bedroom door Yosef said; "I hope you enjoyed your screw," and he was gone.

Taking a deep breath Angelique knew then just how angry Yosef was. Not wanting to piss off Yosef further she showered, dressed and joined him. He was very protective of her; loved her true but they were not together. She was sharing her bed with someone else.

Not apologizing for what he did, when Angelique sat down beside him he said; "those are the numbers."

Looking at the numbers Angelique said; "Yosef, these figures cannot be accurate. What you're telling me with these numbers cannot be real. This is the annihilation of earth. Nothing will survive," Angelique said alarmingly.

"No"

"Yosef"

"Lava is rising Angelique. We've had our warnings and nothing. The different sink holes around the globe. The Earth isn't farting, she's collapsing, ending life as we know it."

"Rebirth"

"Yes"

"How do we stop this?"

"We cannot. We caused this on ourselves. We drill and drill, take and take without replacing. One day everything would eventually come to a foot, and that time is now. We've drilled so far down that we've eroded and or we are eroding earth's inner core. Right now there is no safe distance between the earth's core and humans anymore."

"The greed of man?"

"Yes"

Going over the numbers with Yosef again with a fine tooth comb Angelique could not believe what was happening. She could not believe Earth was coming to an end.

"Is the ring of fire expanding?"

"That's what we are going to find out."

"And the gateway to hell; are the fires flaring or are they stabilized for now?"

"I do not know."

"We have to know Yosef because these gateways connect forming a triangle with Pennsylvania being the furthest point."

"For now, our focus is on the Americas and the Caribbean."

"The major continental shift yet again?"

"More devastating than that of the bible of man; at least the stories of the bible anyway."

"Yosef"

"I know the records of men are false Angelique, but this is not false. Humans take and cannot replace. When we do replace, we replace false; inorganic because the few place and value money over life; the lives of humanity on a whole."

"We are our own worst enemies and time has caught up to man."

"No, man has caught up to the time of their own destruction. We don't think of our future and future generations Angelique. We don't preserve or even think of preservation, so this is the cost of it all. We take all today and leave tomorrow barren."

"Yosef"

As if knowing what Angelique was going to say he said; "there is no borrowed time Angelique. No one can borrow time you know that. As humans, we cannot live for today and leave tomorrow dry and barren. Tomorrow is a part of our lives and tomorrow does come. Tomorrow cannot stop coming or living despite what some say and think because tomorrow is guaranteed. We are the ones to take our tomorrow from us today."

"Then what do we do?"

"Gather the facts and present them truthfully."

"But will they listen?"

"No, the greed of man; humans will once again take precedence over the lives of the many."

"All it takes is one hole."

"I know." He was scared; uncertain, but what could he do? Man had proven time and time again that money and power was more important than the well being of this earth, and life as we know it on this planet.

War and strife was man's main commission – whatever strife they could cause; whatever destruction they could bring upon this earth. Man had to keep death alive hence death is preached; taught by the masses.

Many did not think of peaceful resolutions to problems. Instead, their peaceful resolutions were creating; designing and implementing destructive artillery that destroyed human and earthly life including the trees, the ground and waterways. Many designed diseases and chemical weapons to kill each other and the life of Earth; the planet they live in. In all they did, they did not think of their home and the instability they caused in the lives of all.

No one thinks of life that life is not only human (s); life is the air we breathe, water we drink; food that we eat.

"Yosef you are a wonderful man and we will find a way to solve this", trying to reassure him not to give up.

"How Angelique? How do we fix this? Explosives cannot help. Water who knows. Man; us as humans have and has damaged this planet beyond repair. Now we cannot sustain and maintain ourselves. Once the glaciers are gone, that's it for humans. In all that we talk and do, none has found viable solutions to fix the melting of our glaciers. Humans damage but cannot truly repair Angelique."

"I get what you are saying Yosef, but everything have and has a solution."

"This solution is the annihilation of humanity Angel. Man has done too much wickedness, and earth isn't going to repair herself with vile humans in her. We've taken away too much from her without giving back true and clean."

"I know what you are saying Yosef but are humans so far gone that we cannot fix this?"

"We can't Angel. We use the land and waterways as our dumping ground; our killing fields. Now tell me how much more death can one planet take; survive?"

"Yeah," and she rests her head on the back of her chair. She knew what Yosef said was correct but why did men; the male species of this realm cause so much chaos here on earth? Was power and control so important to them that they had to destroy it all? Why couldn't they learn from past civilizations, civilizations that were wiped off the earth? These things humans knew; spoke about but yet, neglect the facts before them; think it could not and cannot happen again.

Were humans that linear that they could not see the value of life; all life?

Were they that linear that death has become their God; so they had to kill; destroy all in their path to keep death alive?

Thinking of her parents Angelique sent them a quick text. They had to know she was okay and she made sure they knew that. Not thinking of Brent she thought of her family. How she was going to save them from all of this.

Going to Hawaii for three months she and Yosef came up empty. Everything they did came back negative. Hawaii was not the source. Reading the text from Brent she closed her eyes. He missed her, but he wanted to move on sexually and she told him it was fine. She could not keep him to her because they were sex and not in an exclusive relationship. He needed his freedom and Angelique gave it to him without regret or a second thought.

She was enroute to Guam with Yosef but was side tracked. They had to return to North America. A massive earthquake threatened to split Mexico from California. There was no hiccup or belch, just a quake out of the blue at the bottom of the sea. There were casualties and water flooded many areas; townships.

"Oh my God," was all Angelique could say as she and Yosef flew over the affected area in their private jet.

"Angel"

"Look," pointing to the split in the ocean; sea but Yosef could not see what she was seeing. His sight was not clear as hers. She saw the signs but he couldn't.

"There's nothing there."

"There is something there. That thin line as if the water is going back into the sea."

"Baby, I'm sorry I can't see anything."

"Yosef, she is going to explode worse than a thousand atomic bombs combined. The anger, the force that is being built up. We have to get the people out of there. If she blows, California will sink; be no more."

"We need concrete evidence Angel. We can't just evacuate everyone; we have to compile the data and give it to the proper authorities."

"Yeah, and as usual they are going to ignore the signs; our data, and give all the bullshit excuses about it's not economically feasible, spacing and so much more. I know the excuses Yosef and so do you."

"Baby, if I could change things I would but I can't. All I can do is give them the facts; data and hope that they will act; do something."

Working tireously for three weeks, Yosef and Angelique compiled data after data. They had the pictures; everything and sure enough their work was in vain.

"Yosef, you know my hands are tied. I can't evacuate the people. Have you considered the cost or even where we are going to house these people?"

"Gary"

"I know you mean well but I need specifics. I need to know if this gateway or plate is going to erupt within the next forty eight hours, the next week, the next year or so, and you cannot tell me this. I trust you, but I need surety; one hundred percent surety and accuracy that this gateway and or plate are going to rupture in forty eight hours, a day, two weeks and you cannot give me what I need."

"What about the lives?"

"I am thinking about the lives Yosef. I am also thinking about the economics of it all. What if you are wrong? What if this is just an hiccup like Professor Steinburg said?"

"You went to Charlie?"

"No, he came to us. I trust you Yosef but I can't evacuate people based on unsurety time wise. I need a specific timeline. Millions of people are affected not to mention hundreds of millions in Africa and Europe combined. Who knows how hard this eruption will affect them. I have to think Yosef. Like Charlie said, Pennsylvania is the furthest point when it comes to the gateways of hell."

"And I'm not thinking,' retorted Yosef. 'Yes Pennsylvania is the furthest point, but each plate connects; has a rippling effect."

"I know you're thinking but leave the politics to me."

"Ya, politics, but what about the data I've given you?"

"Like I said Yosef, I need a specific time or timeline when this eruption will begin."

"A specific timeline that no one can give you."

"So in the mean time we wait; play the waiting game."

"And hope it's not too late right," supplied Yosef.

"Yes"

"Gary"

"Go home Yosef, you're tired." Gary did not want to hear anymore. He had too much on his plate to think about Mother Earth erupting on a catastrophic scale. And although he trusted Yosef, Charlie's theory was the only viable one. Earth was farting; passing gas. She needed to pass these gases due to man and the pollutants they disbursed in her daily. Too much green house gases were being released into the air coupled with the eroding of the glaciers.

"Gary"

"Go home," and Gary opened the door and left; leaving Yosef to stare after him.

Going home Yosef threw his briefcase and data on the sofa. He could not believe Gary did not want to evacuate the people, nor inform them of the impending danger to California, Mexico, parts of Canada and parts of Europe including the Caribbean.

"Hey"

"He will not evacuate or notify the people of the different lands of the impending danger."

"Yosef you did your best."

"My best was not good enough Angel. He wants a specific timeline of when Mother Earth is going to explode, but I could not give it to him."

"Yosef you did the best you could."

"What if there is something we overlooked; something we are missing Angel?" Doubting himself and the data they gathered.

"Yosef stop. You've never second guessed yourself before, so don't start now."

"Angel, I just want those people to be safe."

"Then pray that Mother Earth have a change of heart. Baby, no one has ever evacuated people on three different continents before. Think, where are they going to put these people?"

"I don't know Angel, but the least they, the authorities at be can do is give the people a fighting chance."

"You know they won't. It's only when the eruption starts that they will be running around like a chicken without a head gathering the different scientists together to come up with a hurried and impractical solution to fix this."

"I know,' pulling Angelique into his arms and hugging her. 'Thank you for being here."

"You're welcome. Now I have to go."

"Please don't."

"Yosef"

"I mean it."

"Yosef, it's best if I do. Besides, dinner is in the oven." Smiling up at him.

"You're going to see him?"

"Yosef my personal life," coming out of his arms and he pulled her back to him. He did not want to let her go and he didn't.

"I don't want you seeing him."

"I know, but it's not him I am going to see. I just want to spend time with my mother my way via Skype."

"You can do that here."

"Yes I can, but I don't want her to get the wrong impression or idea of us Yosef."

"Yeah," smiling ruefully at Angelique.

"Yeah,' tiptoeing and kissing Yosef on the nose. 'Now go wash up and have dinner. I will call my mother from your office," giving him his heart's desire. Today had been a hard blow for him. He thought Gary would at least consider the happenings of Mother Earth as well as his findings; data, but that was not to be. Now he had to pray that all will be well but he knew differently. Mother Earth was tired; tired of the evils in her, tired of the pain; death toll; war and strife.

"Thank you and be careful, my office is a mess."

"What else is new with you Mr. Workaholic and Paper and Notes Everywhere," and he smiled. He was happy she was going to spend the night. Now they could talk and see what course of action they must take. They had to prepare for the worst; had to have an action plan.

"You get me."

"I will always get you Yosef. You are dedicated and passionate about what you do."

"True"

"You know what go because I am swelling your head."

"It's been a long time since you've swelled my head."

"True," and she pulled out of his arms. Going to his office she shook her head because Yosef did have papers everywhere. Every page of data was placed strategically. Every page meant something. Every page had its own place. Looking at everything Angelique carefully stepped her way to Yosef's computer. Turning it on she logged into his computer. Seeing the picture of her and Yosef on an expedition brought back memories, memories that showed how they both relied on each other, trusted each other and respected each other. Calling her mother Angelique got her on the first ring.

"You are months late."

"Sorry mom but been busy."

"Earth sinking?"

"It seems so."

"Man tampering with God's universe. When will they stop child?"

"I don't know."

"That bad."

"It seems, but we will pull through this. Now, how is the house?"

"Fine. We've been having way more than usual rain and many people are flooded out."

"But your house is safe?"

"Yes. The levy is holding to so far."

"And granny?"

"She's fine. She's here with me with my father."

"Kiss them both for me."

"I will. How's Yosef?"

"He's fine."

"More like stressed."

"That too. Did you get the solar panels added to the house like I've asked you to?" Making small talk with her mother but Angelique knew her mother knew all the happenings of Mother Earth. She was that in tune with Earth. It was only a matter of time before Mother Earth explode in full anger.

"Yes"

"Good"

"Baby what's going on because you are scaring me?"

"I know and I am sorry, but you know me when it comes to you."

"Yes I do. Have you been looking into the tornadoes here?"

"No. Jamaican tornadoes are not that severe."

"The one in Negril was. It devastated the area; left many homeless and dead. Times are changing child, times are changing; too much flooding, disasters; killings worldwide."

"Yes, but we as humans have and has contributed to the decay and erosion of earth's natural fault lines."

"We need these resources baby."

"Mama, we need resources yes but at what cost to humans lives? Bombs and ammunition we do not need but yet, man; humans build to destroy instead of building to preserve."

"Baby men are wicked creatures you know that. From they took Eve out of God's kingdom, they've done nothing but war and kill; destroy the natural habitat of this earth. And some women are no better either. Now look at the chaos on earth due to their lies; false teachings they spread globally. Now go back to man's so called holy book; who committed the first murder?"

"Man; more specifically Cain," Angelique answered.

"Now tell me, what makes man the superior race; the head of anyone? Are their nature not murderous; engrained in death; their DNA? Now tell me, if man was the first to commit murder according to man's so called holy book; what makes Man a God? Is it man that is sustaining humanity here on earth, is it not Mother; Mother Earth; Woman? So now tell me this; can man bring forth life without the aid of a female but yet, Earth need not a male to bring forth life; give birth. So, should we not respect Earth and give thanks to God that he left Mother; Mother Earth for us to enjoy; keep us safe from harm?"

"True, but mom; why do man have to put themselves above God and all?"

"Control, greed, power. Now look at the different stories and myths of man. Are they not all the same? Do men not kill? Even the Gods of Men kill. So how can life live amongst the dead; fathers?"

"I don't know."

"Baby we cannot put ourselves above God. It cannot work hence the people of this earth is corrupt and destructive.

Man cannot be God because men are not true. They disrupt the natural balance in life with their lies and deceit. Look Baby Girl, evil is contained here on earth. Evil cannot go anyplace else to kill human flesh or spiritual flesh; life. <u>So in all that God did, he made sure evil is contained here on earth but man; humans do not know this.</u> In all that humans do, they cannot flee earth to go and pollute another planet or domain. God and Death will never permit this. Know that what is not of God is of Death; belongs to Death. "

"I didn't know these things."

"Well now you do. Earth need to purge herself baby and all acts of nature is due to humans and their greed; sins."

"But when will humans learn Maa? Can they not see they are hurting self and taking life away from them? Can they not see the good in self and this earth?"

"Not all can or will learn child. Remember all that we've been given is false information to live by and go by. Humans know not the truth, so the cycle of death continues." *(Time Will Tell, Robert Nesta Marley aka Bob Marley and Lions Skip Marley).*

"But for a time."

"No, not for a time but forever, or until man; humans change from their lying and deceitful ways and accept the full and true truth of life. Now with all that said, how's Brent?"

"We are no longer seeing each other. Besides, it was just sex."

"And sex is no reason to be with a man Angelique, you know this."

"But I needed it mother."

"You did not needed it,' Angelique's mother barked. 'You do not add to the chaos and nastiness of this planet."

"Mom I know what you are saying, but I did need it."

"No you did not. You did wrong. You stay and work out your problems, you do not run from them no matter your hurt and pain including disappointments. Baby girl, you learn from your failures and disappointments."

"Mom I wanted this so badly."

"But was this what you truly needed at the time baby girl? Needs and wants are two different things. You have to facture in preparedness, your financial stability, a home, your living and livity including lifestyle."

"Mom my world was perfect."

"But yet, you left that perfect world; could not cope with your own insecurities in your perfect world."

"Because it became tainted," Angelique barked at her mother.

"Then if it was tainted, you tainted it because nothing can be impure or tainted in a perfect world."

"Mom," and Angelique cried. She was still hurting. The pain of the past was too much for her even now.

"It's okay I am here. Talk, talk and do more talking. Now I have to go."

"So soon?"

"Yes because you are not in your office, and that man has paper everywhere."

"Yes he does," smiling.

"Where to next?"

"I want and need to come see you."

"Nope, go solve the world's problem because I need saving."

"Mom"

"I mean it baby. Mama Earth is pissed, and I need reassurance from her that everything is going to be okay. You are the key to life baby so truly live."

"I don't want to go there Mama."

"But yet you have to. Do not let your fair take you from the truth ever again because you are the truth."

"Thanks mom. You know you are truly loved."

"Yes I do, hence you make sure I am well taken care of."

"Got to because life is worth it."

"All the time, now stay safe and go. Kiss messy boy for me."

"I will," smiling and her mother was gone. Angelique's mother knew Yosef to a T. She could not understand why he had such a great need for paper, and to have paper everywhere.

"You know she will be okay."

"I know she will be Mama. She has who she needs with her."

"Then fear not for her. Let her live."

"She is now."

Leaving Yosef's office she found him lying down in his bedroom. Bending she kissed him on the cheek. "That's from my mother."

"Tell her thank you the next time you speak to her."

"I will. Tired?"

"Yes"

"Then get some rest; sleep," but Yosef did not want sleep. He wanted and needed to talk to her and he did.

"Angel I am truly sorry you know."

"I know," looking in his eyes she saw the hurt and pain in them. Lowering her head she kissed him. She needed to do that for some strange reason. She did not want him to hurt no more. The pain was too great for him.

Feeling the warmth and truth of Yosef, he pulled her to lay atop him. Discarding her clothes while she was atop him Yosef rolled her beneath him, and *"Let Her Go" by Christopher Martin began to play.* He had wanted Angelique; wanted her so badly and he was having her. He needed no barriers between them and there was none. Angelique was not holding anything back from him. She was freely giving to him, and he gladly accepted her freedom and warmth; truth.

Angelique was home and he could not let her go. His life was no longer empty. His bed was no longer empty. His yearning, cravings at nights as he laid in the dark and cried was now fulfilled. His baby, life partner, need was back and he intended on making her stay in his life forevermore.

His snow and cold filled days was once again warm; perfect because his perfection was back in his life.

"Yosef"

"Say nothing, let me enjoy you."

"Oh my God Yosef," and she screamed in pleasure. Consummating the union Angelique clung to him. She was in paradise again and she was enjoying every pleasure paradise gave her. Kissing Angelique she received his moans in a strong kiss.

"Thank you, I need that."

"I know. The pain was too much for you."

"Yes," smiling down at Angelique.

Cuddled to Angelique he lazily got out of bed early the next morning. Making her coffee he woke her by pulling the sheet to her butt and exposing her back. Kissing her awake she moaned in pleasure. She knew coffee was ready and she turned on her back exposing her naked breasts. Everything about her body, thoughts, work was perfect;

that perfect body that haunted Yosef at nights. That perfect body that commanded his body in a way no other could; now she was back in his bed and he was going to make sure she never leave out again. Lowering his head he tasted of her nipple and felt it stiffen in his mouth.

"My coffee is going to get cold," smiling.

"Let it," and he basked in her beauty; the warmth of her love yet again.

She could not have her coffee because his juice; touch and warmth was too good, toxic in a good way. Pumping his beloved he came and said; "please don't ever let me go."

"Yosef"

"Angel, I can't lose you again."

"I know."

"Then commit; let's commit to each other."

"I can't right now Yosef. I need something different."

"Then let me give it to you; let me give you that something different."

"Yosef"

"Angelique"

"You know what, let me make you breakfast." She wasn't ready to bring up the past and Yosef knew that. The past did hurt him as well as her, and he had to give her time; her space to come to him and talk. They both needed healing and were avoiding the healing process.

Getting out of bed she went to take a shower and Yosef joined her. It's been a long time since they showered together or did anything together a part from work.

Touching his body under the water he knew what she wanted. He had felt the heat of her body dancing with his. He could not say no, he could not resist; she was too tempting, too hot, too enticing; too natural. She was that natural and kind. Had an exceptional relationship with her family especially her mother. Resting her body on the wall Yosef delved into her lava once again. Fulfilling her needs and his desire, he came; exploded within her. Holding her under the water he was tired. He had not ejaculated like that in a long while.

"I tired you out."

"Yes. It's been a long time since I've ejaculated that fierce in you."

"I know but your body needed it. I needed it and it was awesome."

"Yeah"

"Yeah," kissing Angelique and he burst out laughing.

"Missed this?"

"Yes"

"So why threaten him?"

"Jealousy, seeing the way you were so happy with him; him satisfying you sexually. I wanted and needed to be the only one in your life sexually Angel. I wanted and needed to make you scream out in ecstatic bliss. I wanted and needed to be the only one to touch you, but you had him.' He was getting upset now. 'You had him in you. You had him fucking you. I should have been the one," he barked.

"Yosef"

"No don't because I don't want to forgive you for banging him and enjoying it."

"And her?"

"Could not satisfy me like you, but he satisfied you."

"Not like you. You're different Yosef. He was sex. And please don't give me a lecture, my mother already did that."

"Good. Now I am starving."

"Yeah, yeah, yeah." And Angelique left him in the water.

Preparing a hearty breakfast for the both of them. Both lovers went back to bed. Laying there naked Yosef went between her legs.

"Yosef don't do that."

"I need to Angelique. I need to."

"Yosef," and she tried to move but could not. Yosef had held her too tight. Her legs were wide open and he had his head touching her vagina. He was like a baby wanting to go back home. He was on his back and she was on her back and he said; "if I could go up there and be our child for you Angelique I would, but I cannot bring her back. I know you blame me for losing our daughter, but I am so sorry,' and he cried. 'I am so sorry I can't be her, so sorry I can't bring her back to us for you to truly love me again. I drove you out of my life, and I am sorry, so sorry."

Hearing those words Angelique said; "Yosef please come from between my legs that way."

"I want to stay here and be our daughter for you; for us Angelique."

"I know, but you can't. Now come up and lay on my chest," and he did.

"Angelique I love you true."

"I know and it was wrong of me to blame you. It was wrong of me to hurt you by leaving. Yosef you're a wonderful, caring, kind, truthful, truly giving man. You're smart, beautiful, my perfect man. I am sorry I tainted you. It's like I did not know how to handle loss; our loss, and it was easy to blame you so I did. Tragedy wasn't supposed to happen to us. I could not accept tragedy or the truth of losing our child."

"Baby I know and I wanted to fix it all for us."

"But we can't fix it all Yosef. Some things happen in life to make us stronger not weaker. I became weak and shut you out; left and for that, I am truly sorry."

"Our world was perfect Angelique. Like you said; tragedy wasn't supposed to enter into our perfect world."

"But it did and neither one of us more so me, did not know how to handle it."

"And now?"

"Glad you are still in my life and that I am working with you still. Right now I am where I truly need to be."

"And commitment Angelique?"

"You have it."

"Good because there will be no separation or having casual sex or sex with anyone apart from me."

"You have my word."

"But you are scared?"

"Yes, but we have to go."

"You don't want to go there?"

"No, but we have to."

"Then take my hand,' and she did. 'We will protect each other."

"Thank you."

"You're welcome," getting off Angelique she knew what was about to happen. They had both gotten each other a commitment ring.

"I'm ready, have always been ready Angelique."

"Yosef I'm scared."

"Why"

"I don't know."

"You have feelings for him?"

"No"

"Angelique you're a part of my world; my everything."

"I know."

"Then don't be scared. Like you I need children. I am not afraid to have them. I need all my children to come from you and no one else but you."

"But she said she was pregnant."

"And the DNA test came back negative Angelique. I know my body. I know how it reacts. I definitely know my sperm."

"And this morning in the shower?"

"You tell me," and she smiled at him. Yosef had always protected her; did everything with her and now she was back. Getting the rings he put her ring on and she did his. No words were exchanged and the two held each other in each other's arms. Sleeping for a few hours the two's email from both sides of the family said; "it's about time and congratulations."

"We are official."

"Yes we are official," kissing Angelique. His world was now complete because the love he'd lost was now home.

Going to Guam two weeks later Angelique got the devastating news. A crater opened up in Kingston, Jamaica about two football fields in length. Mother Nature struck without warning now ***Black Mother Prays. Tarrus Riley ft Jimmy Riley.*** Mother Nature was out for revenge and she started in a place where man would not look; in the Caribbean; the epicentre of Judah; the Jews.

Black Mother had to pray for her own now because many did turn from life; gave up their own and home for naught.

Judah's falling; Judah's fallen; now death stalked Israel; the US; United States of America.

Death consumes, walk, talk now devours; soon to devour.

As hot water rise from beneath the lava came; death came. He wails, "Dear God not me, not my family, not my land," but it was too late. Their pleas fell on deaf ears. Nature came, took; left all for dead.

"Yosef"

"Baby your family will be fine. They know what to do."

"Yosef I know, but two football fields. Dear God the island is sinking beneath them and the people have not the slightest clue."

"But you said it was going to happen, it's been a long time coming. People do not preserve, nor do they think of their future."

"Ya"

"Angelique, all the fault lines connect and intersect in some way."

"Baby I know. I'm just thinking of Noah's Ark. This great disaster that's going to take the lives of billions. Yosef, and she ran to the railing, held on and vomited at sea."

Going by Angelique's side Yosef put his hand around her; holding on to her. "I'll be fine," and she vomited again.

"Sulphur?"

"Yes, too much."

"Angelique"

"We have to go back Yosef. We cannot stay."

"We need to find the truth Angelique."

"Not on this day."

"Can we at least take samples?"

"I did already."

"I have to dive."

"No. She will not permit you. She's protecting us."

"Angelique"

"Heed her cries and warnings Yosef. You are a part of my world too."

"But you were scared to come here."

"Yes because I did you wrong. Now that we have made amends, and have a clean slate she will protect us at all cost."

"Thank you."

"You're welcome," he heard. He had never heard the voice of life before and now he did, and by the next day Angelique and Yosef was gone. Going back home the samples Angelique took turned black; as if black stone.

"What happened?"

"I don't know." Calling her mother she heard, "put them with the rest, demandingly."

"Mama"

"Put them with the rest. You are not responsible for the sins of man. She's hurting. She gave good; humans were the ones to return bad; give her all of their nastiness and pain. Her tears are no longer clear but black, so put them all where they belong. Put them with death in the vault of death. She can no longer maintain and sustain the wicked and evil of this world."

"Mom"

"Do not defy her Yosef. Put them with the rest," and they did. Every last sample they took they put with the rest and securely locked the vault of Sin and Death.

The darkness of earth was coming together and they had to secure all who needed to be secured. Earth needed to replenish herself but not in an evil way, but in a good way. Humans did explore but with all the exploring, the lies came, the wars came, the depleting of her resources came, the bombs and ammunition came, the hatred and sin came. Mountains of death came because the sins of men; humans were more than mountainous. The lies of men; humans could no longer be contained. Humans had to die; Mother Earth had to do her part by withdrawing herself from her lying and deceitful children; those who share her physical DNA.

Man and land reflect each other but when it came to land, men; humans destroy it all. Greed and profit were there ultimate gain.

Man did gain it all only to lose it all in the end.

Profit overshadowed life

Hate overshadowed life

War overshadowed life

Man, put and value money above life

Man, take life each and every day

Hence death came; became a part of man's DNA; their corrupt household; self.

Kneeling before Angelique Yosef kissed her stomach. He wanted and needed this child. This child represented more than a bond between them. This child represented the old and the new.

Closing her eyes Angelique ran her fingers through his hair. He was a weird man to her but she enjoyed his weirdness.

"Angelique"

She knew what he wanted and she made him take his fill of her. He wanted sex and he got it. Nothing mattered to him right now. Angelique was with him, she was going to have his child. Nothing could spoil his mood.

"Oh my God, what's going on?" Someone screamed. The sink hole was expanding and hot water and lava began to spew in the air. Devastation was now on land and no one could save themselves. All that man did to destroy earth had come full throttle and blast before them.

Resting in Angelique's arms Yosef lazily answered Angelique's cell phone.

"Mom what's going on?"

"Get you and your family to safety now."

"Mom"

"Now Yosef,' she barked. 'They have forty eight hours after that all will be lost. I cannot save them or guarantee their safety here on earth."

"Mom all of my family are all over the globe."

"You know the portals Yosef. So do they, use them."

"Yes mam," and he hung up.

"Time to go?"

"Yes"

"The eruption has begun?"

"Yes," and at that moment Gary braist for the worst.
Yosef was right, his data was correct, now he did not know what to do to save humanity.

Scrambling to call Yosef he got a busy signal. All his people did to override the busy signal failed. Not even Google Map and Google Earth could locate them. It was as if they disappeared off the face of the planet.

Sitting up in bed Angelique looked at Yosef. "Billions are going to die," and *Time Will Tell by Bob Marley began to play. Time now played for all of humanity.*

"I know but there is absolutely nothing we can do about this Angelique. Man caused this on themselves. The remnants that are left must find home; shelter, and so must we. We cannot wait until the last minute lest we be caught up in this."

"Yosef"

"I am not taking any chances Angelique. You're pregnant and I have to secure my family. I will not save them because there is no room in the Ark for them. I've been trying for years and was ignored, called a quack, demented and other derogatory names. Every piece of data we gathered; had, we gave to the proper authorities and they brushed them aside. So let them handle the consequences now. Our priorities lie elsewhere."

"Yosef I know all these things, but I can't help not thinking about what's to come; happen to them."

"You have to stop thinking about it because all the warning signs were there. Humans chose to ignore them. Many played the game; got caught up in the lies and distraction. We can't, so let's go. I will not lose my place and family for anyone Angelique. My family heeded the warning signs; were instrumental in the creation of this new earth. I need better for us; a better way and life and this is it."

"I know Yosef."

"So don't think of them. Think of us for a change, and yes, be selfish this once for me. We are saved. We heeded Earth's cry. She helped us with our new home. So let's go."

"Can't be selfish, but I will think of us," and he kissed her naked breast.

Getting his cell phone, he sent out the first beacon. Waiting twenty minutes the second beacon was sent from Angelique's cell phone and forty eighty hours later they got the message all was accounted for. Absolutely nothing was left behind. All those that had to be in New Earth was in New Earth.

"Let's go Angelique."

"Baby"

"No second thoughts Angelique," and Yosef pulled her to him.

Decontaminating mind, body and soul two lovers were gone to a different world leaving billions of people behind.

The saved were already in New Earth. All that was left were the left behinds; those that did not heed the call; her, the bell of life ringing; calling, calling them, warning them, pleading with them to prepare; get on the Ark of safety truth. ***People Get Ready, Curtis Mayfield and the Impressions. Sam Cooke, A Change Gone Come, this book, Rise Goes Up, My Heart to Heart with Lovey 2017, No Feel, Blackman Redemption and so much more.***

Closing their eyes and holding each other, Angelique kissed Yosef's hand and cuddled closer to him. Darkness was now on earth because darkness was unleashed on humanity. None would be saved because in all they did; they did Mother Earth wrong. There was no bargaining for humanity. All that bargained for them lost their lives because humans refused to change their dirty ways. They could not see their wrongs; the errors of their ways. Reaching home to the delight of friends and family all was glad because they now had a new start without the violence and crime of old earth.

All that was left behind. Peace was now on the land and it was not all nations that were with them. In this earth there was no racism, no colour of skin, religion. All had the same language, the same hue; hair type, eye colour of green; starburst green and blue combined. There was no cause to hate or fight, lie and deceive because all was well. This was a new earth and a new beginning for the chosen few. Earth did show man and mankind signs and wonders and many played the fool, could not put those signs and wonders together; now billions would lose their life due to ignorance; not listening and heeding the call of the righteous; those of the truth.

Yosef and Angelique had made it to New Earth but those that were left behind on old earth were not so lucky. The darkness came and one by one they died. Mother Earth came together with all her elements and faded away to dust.

Earth was now a water planet. The fire in her raged; could not be cooled for a time times time. All that were above was submerged under water, and the lava of the water disintegrated all in its path. It was as if humans never existed; walked the face of the earth. Not one remnant of the old or past civilization was left on earth. Everything was truly gone. Humans wanted death so they got death. Those who were of life now had life; were safely away from the children of death. They wept no more; had no reason to weep because all was well. Tomorrow did come for the wicked and evil. But in all I say; write, what about you; your tomorrow?

Truly think and I dedicate ***Tomorrow and It Would Be You by Pieter T*** to all of you.

MLG